Grimm's Fairy Tales

For Auntie Giovanna
S.P.

For Smilla
C.J.

ORCHARD BOOKS
338 Euston Road, London NW1 3BH
Orchard Books Australia
Level 17/207 Kent Street, Sydney, NSW 2000

This text was first published in the form of a gift collection called
The Sleeping Princess by Orchard Books in 2002

This edition first published in hardback in 2012
First paperback publication in 2013

ISBN 978 1 40830 835 6 (hardback)
ISBN 978 1 40830 836 3 (paperback)

Text © Saviour Pirotta 2002
Illustrations © Cecilia Johansson 2012

The rights of Saviour Pirotta to be identified as the author and
Cecilia Johansson to be identified as the illustrator of this work
have been asserted by them in accordance
with the Copyright, Designs and Patents Act, 1988.

A CIP catalogue record for this book is available
from the British Library.

1 3 5 7 9 10 8 6 4 2 (hardback)
1 3 5 7 9 10 8 6 4 2 (paperback)

Printed in China

Orchard Books is a division of Hachette Children's Books,
an Hachette UK company.
www.hachette.co.uk

Grimm's Fairy Tales

Rapunzel

Written by Saviour Pirotta

Illustrated by Cecilia Johansson

ORCHARD

A long time ago there was a couple who very much wanted a child. And now, after many years, their wish was to come true!

They lived in a small cottage right next to a magnificent garden that belonged to a wicked witch.

One day, the woman looked out of
her back window and spied a delicious
herb called rapunzel, growing in the
witch's garden.

The woman wanted nothing else but to eat a big bowl of it. So her husband climbed over the garden wall and filled a basket with fresh rapunzel leaves.

His wife was delighted. She made a salad
with them and ate it.

No sooner had she finished eating
than she looked out of the window and
wished for some more.

The husband had no choice but to
creep into the witch's garden once again.
But this time the witch caught him.

"How dare you steal my rapunzel?"
roared the witch, who'd been lying in wait.

"Forgive me, I beg you," said the husband, shaking. "The herb is for my wife who is expecting a child."

"In that case," said the witch, "you can have as much of the herb as you want. But only on one condition . . .

. . . when your child is born you must give it to me."

The husband was so terrified of the
witch, he agreed right away.

Then he returned
home and gave his
wife the rapunzel.

A few months later the baby was born. It was a girl, and as soon as she uttered her first cry, the witch appeared.

The parents begged in vain to keep their daughter. "A promise is a promise," shrieked the witch. She wrapped the child in a shawl, called her Rapunzel after the herb, and took her away.

Rapunzel grew up to be a beautiful girl with long hair that shone like spun gold.

When Rapunzel was
twelve years old,
the witch locked her up
in a tower, deep in the
middle of a thick forest.

"No one will find
you here, my pretty,"
she cackled. "You'll
stay with me for ever."

The tower had no door, so when the witch
wanted to come in, she would stand outside
and call:

"Rapunzel, Rapunzel,
Sweet and fair,
Granny is here,
Let down your hair."

Then Rapunzel would lean out of the window so her long tresses would tumble down to the ground. The witch would grab her hair like a rope and very slowly climb up!

One day, a prince was riding through
the forest. The prince heard Rapunzel singing
and wanted to meet her at the window.

He tried in vain to find a way into the tower. There was no door or ladder. "There must be a way in and out of this place," he thought. "I shall hide nearby until someone comes."

At suppertime, the witch appeared with
some food for Rapunzel. She stood at the foot
of the tower and called:

"Rapunzel, Rapunzel,
Sweet and fair,
Granny is here,
Let down your hair."

When the witch left, the prince stood under
the tower, and, with his heart beating wildly
in his chest, called out the same words.

Down tumbled the golden tresses, and up climbed the prince. What a shock Rapunzel had! But the prince started to talk to her and his gentle voice soothed away her fears.

"Run away with me," he said. "I love you and shall make you my queen."

To help Rapunzel escape, the prince brought her a piece of silk every night. Rapunzel used the pieces to weave a long ladder.

It was nearly long enough to reach the ground when Rapunzel made a terrible mistake.

"Why do you take so long to climb up my hair?" Rapunzel asked the witch one night. "My prince is with me in a moment."

"A prince?" roared the witch. In a fit of rage, she seized a pair of scissors and lopped off Rapunzel's long locks.

Then she chanted a magic spell and threw Rapunzel into a desert.

That night the witch fastened Rapunzel's
chopped-off hair to a hook by the window.

Shortly after midnight, the prince arrived with one last piece of silk. He called out in his usual way.

Down tumbled the tresses . . .

. . . and up climbed the prince.

He got such a shock when he saw the witch,
he fell backwards out of the window.

When he landed in the bushes below, the
thorns pierced his eyes and made him blind.

For years, the prince wandered around the
forest, too miserable without Rapunzel to care
about the loss of his sight.

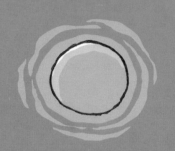

Then, one day, he stumbled onto soft, desert lands.

The sun was blazing and his mind started to wander. Was that a voice he could hear in the wilderness? It sounded so much like his beloved Rapunzel.

He stood and listened. Yes, it was Rapunzel!

He called out to her and they fell into each other's arms. Rapunzel's tears of joy rained down on the prince's eyes and in an instant he could see again, clear as day.

Rapunzel and the prince travelled back to his father's kingdom. There they married, and lived happily ever after.